WHO WANTS
Arthur?

Library of Congress Cataloging-in-Publication Data

Graham, Amanda, 1961-
   Who wants Arthur?

   (A Quality time book)
   Rev. ed. of: Arthur.
   Summary: Arthur, a dog in a pet store waiting to be
adopted, takes on the identities of other animals he
thinks might be more appealing, until discovering that
he can be a success as himself.
   [1. Dogs—Fiction.   2. Pets—Fiction.   3. Individual-
ity—Fiction]   I. Gynell, Donna, ill.   II. Graham,
Amanda, 1961-   .   Arthur.   III. Title.
PZ7.G75166Wh   1987   [E]   86-42812
ISBN 1-55532-178-X
ISBN 1-55532-153-4 (lib. bdg.)

North American edition first published in 1987 by

Gareth Stevens, Inc.
7317 West Green Tree Road
Milwaukee, WI 53223, USA

Text copyright © 1984 by Amanda Graham
Illustrations copyright © 1984 by Donna Gynell

First published in Australia as *Arthur* by Era Publications.

Typeset by A-Line Typographers, Milwaukee.
   2   3   4   5   6   7   8   9   92   91   90   89   88

WHO WANTS
Arthur?

Story by Amanda Graham   Pictures by Donna Gynell

Gareth Stevens Publishing
Milwaukee

Arthur was a very ordinary dog.
He lived in Mrs. Humber's Pet Shop
with many other animals.
But Arthur was the **only** dog.
All the other dogs
had been sold, because
dogs were very popular —
all the dogs **except Arthur**.
He was just an ordinary brown dog.
And all he wanted
was a home,
with a pair of old slippers
to chew.

On Monday morning, Mrs. Humber
put some rabbits in the window.

By the end of the day,
the window was empty —
except for Arthur.
Nobody wanted an
ordinary brown dog today.
Everybody wanted rabbits.

So that night,
when all was quiet,
Arthur practiced being
a rabbit.

7

He practiced eating carrots.
He practiced poking out his front teeth
and making his ears
stand up straight.

He practiced very hard,
until he was **sure**
he could be a rabbit.

The next morning, Mrs. Humber
put some snakes in the window.

By the end of the day,
the window was empty —
except for Arthur.
Nobody wanted an
ordinary brown dog,
not even one who acted like a rabbit.
Everybody wanted snakes.

So that night,
when all was quiet,
Arthur practiced being a snake.

He practiced

h i s s i n g

and *slithering*

and *sliding*

and looking cool.

He practiced very hard,
until he was **sure**
he could be a snake.

The next morning, Mrs. Humber
put some fish in the window.

By the end of the day,
the window was empty —
except for Arthur.
Nobody wanted an
ordinary brown dog,
not even one
who acted like a rabbit
and a snake.
Everybody wanted a fish.

So that night,
when all was quiet,
Arthur practiced being a fish.

He practiced *swimming*
and blowing bubbles
and breathing underwater.

He practiced very hard,
until he was **sure**
he could be a fish.

The next morning, Mrs. Humber
put some cats in the window.

By the end of the day,
the window was empty —
except for Arthur.
Nobody wanted an
ordinary brown dog,
not even one who acted
like a **rabbit**
and a **snake**
and a **fish**.
Everybody wanted **cats.**

Arthur felt he would
never find a home
with a pair of old slippers
to chew.

19

The next morning, Mrs. Humber
put the rest of her
pets in the window.

There were two hamsters,
a cage of mice, three canaries,
a blue parakeet, a green frog,
one sleepy lizard,
and Arthur.

Arthur *jumped* on lilypads,

 squeaked,

and *nibbled* cheese.

He *p u r r e d ,*

croaked,

and even tried to **fly**.

By the end of the day,
the window was empty —
except for Arthur.

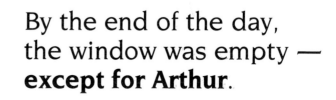

Arthur was all worn out.
He collapsed
in the corner of the window.

Now he was **sure** he would never
find a home,
whether he was
a rabbit,
a snake,
a fish,
a cat,
or a purple, spotted, three-headed
donkey.

Arthur decided that he might as well
be just an ordinary brown dog.

Late that afternoon,
Mrs. Humber was just about
to close the shop.
In came a little girl
with her Grandpa.
"Excuse me," said the Grandpa,
"Melanie tells me that
you have a very
special dog,
who performs all sorts
of tricks."

"The only dog I have,"
replied Mrs. Humber,
"is Arthur."

"**There** he is, Grandpa,
in the window!" cried Melanie.

She rushed to pick up Arthur.
He gave her the
biggest, wettest, doggiest
lick ever.

At last!
Arthur knew he had found a home,

with a pair of old slippers
to chew.